To our children-Jackson, Marlee, Ollie Kai & Finley, who see the magic in this beautiful miraculous world! May you always feel how deeply you are loved.

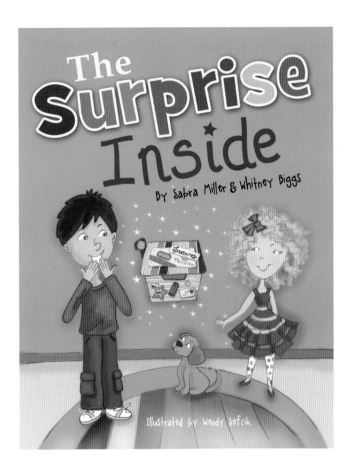

By Sabra Miller and Whitney Biggs

Illustrated by Wendy Sefcik

www.treasuredpassages.com

Published by Treasured Passages

Printed in China, 2012.

First Edition 2012

ISBN: 978-0-9797269-5-8

It was an ordinary end to an ordinary day. As Sam lay tucked into his bed, he thought of the letter he'd received in the mail from his grandparents. It came in a bright yellow envelope and was filled with stickers, gum and a new dollar bill. Sam treasured these treats and carried them into dreamland.

Yes, this was an ordinary end to an ordinary day.
Or was it?

That night Sam had a fabulous dream. He saw BIG letters, small letters, bright envelopes, striped envelopes, all with a story to tell and person to find.

Sam asked one of the letters *"How do you find the person you were written for?"*
The letter giggled and said, *"We just look for their magic mailbox."*
Sam asked, *"Can I have a magic mailbox?"* But before the letter could answer,
Sam woke up. He couldn't wait to tell his mom about his dream so he quickly
got dressed and headed down for breakfast.

When he opened his bedroom door, he couldn't believe what he saw…
his own Magic Mailbox! He looked inside and pulled out
a mysterious note that read…

Sam was thrilled to have a mailbox of his own and raced to look
inside every morning. He didn't always find a treasure waiting for him which
made the days he did even more special. Finally, at the end of the week,
he discovered a gold medal, and attached was a note…

He pinned his medal on his shirt and wore it, along with a smile, all day long.

A week went by and the mailbox remained empty.
But that was OK because Sam was looking forward to going to the
Japanese Festival with his grandparents. His favorite part was trying all the
different foods, and his sister liked getting her face painted like a tiger.

The next morning, when Sam reached into his mailbox,
he pulled out some funny looking sticks with a note…

Later that afternoon,
as Sam was playing,
he heard some rustling
noises in the hall.
"Who's out there?"
Sam yelled.

He peeked out to investigate but saw nothing unusual until he opened his mailbox and found a blue bird's feather, 3 small acorns, and a red shiny marble. These little treasures made him grow curious about his mysterious Treasure Fairy.

The weeks passed quickly and Sam was getting really excited about his upcoming birthday. When the big day arrived he rushed out to see if there were any presents waiting for him. The first place he looked was his mailbox. Inside he found a cupcake eraser with a note attached.

Maybe little sisters are pretty cool after-all, Sam thought.

Over the next few months, Sam sent and received many wonderful letters. He even put his note to Santa in the mailbox. From time to time, he would find surprises from his Treasure Fairy, and he decided to write her a note. He put the note in the mailbox along with his favorite toy car.

The next morning Sam's car and note were gone and in the mailbox was a chocolate kiss.

That night, the Treasure Fairy visited Sam in his dreams!
*"I'm glad to meet you, Treasure Fairy. I love the mailbox you made for me!
Do you visit other children?"* Sam asked.
"I most certainly do," she exclaimed. *"If they wish for a mailbox of their own, then I will
make one, and fill it with treasures. But I must go now, sweet dreams, Sam."*

Tonight, at bedtime, make a WISH for your own mailbox.
Who knows? Maybe you'll see the Treasure Fairy in your dreams,
and if you see her, tell her Sam says *"hello!"*